I, Not I

A Beginning-to-Read Book

Illustrated by Bert Dodson
retold story of The Little Red Hen

NORWOOD HOUSE 🏠 PRESS

DEAR CAREGIVER,

The books in this Beginning-to-Read collection may look somewhat familiar in that the original versions could have been a part of your own early reading experiences. These carefully written texts feature common sight words to provide your child multiple exposures to the words appearing most frequently in written text. These new versions have been updated and the engaging illustrations are highly appealing to a contemporary audience of young readers.

Begin by reading the story to your child, followed by letting him or her read familiar words and soon your child will be able to read the story independently. At each step of the way, be sure to praise your reader's efforts to build his or her confidence as an independent reader. Discuss the pictures and encourage your child to make connections between the story and his or her own life. At the end of the story, you will find reading activities and a word list that will help your child practice and strengthen beginning reading skills. These activities, along with the comprehension questions are aligned to current standards, so reading efforts at home will directly support the instructional goals in the classroom.

Above all, the most important part of the reading experience is to have fun and enjoy it!

Shannon Cannon

Shannon Cannon,
Literacy Consultant

Norwood House Press • www.norwoodhousepress.com
Beginning-to-Read™ is a registered trademark of Norwood House Press.
Illustration and cover design copyright ©2017 by Norwood House Press. All Rights Reserved.

Authorized adapted reprint from the U.S. English language edition, entitled Not I, Not I by Margaret Hillert. Copyright © 2017 Margaret Hillert. Reprinted with permission. All rights reserved. Pearson and Not I, Not I are trademarks, in the US and/or other countries, of Pearson Education, Inc. or its affiliates. This publication is protected by copyright, and prior permission to re-use in any way in any format is required by both Norwood House Press and Pearson Education. This book is authorized in the United States for use in schools and public libraries.

Designer: Lindaanne Donohoe
Editorial Production: Lisa Walsh

Paperback ISBN: 978-1-60357-911-7
The Library of Congress has cataloged the hardcover edition of this book with the following call number: 2016009492

297R-092016
Printed in ShenZhen, Guangdong, China.

Here is a mother.
The mother is little.
The mother is red.

Look here.
Here is a little baby.
The baby is yellow.
It can run and play.

See the yellow baby run.
See it run to Mother.
It said, "Mother, Mother.
I want something."

Mother said, "Come and look.
Help me find something.
Away we go."

Look, look.
Here is something.
Something little.
I can work.
I can make it big.

Oh, oh.
Look here.
One, two, three.
Can you help me?

Not I.
Not I.
Not I.
We can not help.

I can.
I can work.
See it go down here.

Look, look.
See where it is.
It is up.
It is big, big, big.

Can you help?
Can you three help me?
Come and work.

Not I.
Not I.
Not I.
We can not help.

It is funny.
You can not work.
You can not help.
I can work.

Here I go.
Away, away.
Can you come?
Can you help?

Not I.
Not I.
Not I.
We can not help.

See, see.
It is in here.
I can make something.

I can work.
See me work.
I can make
something.

Look here, baby.
It can go in here.
It is for you.

Here it is.
Come and look.
Oh, oh.
Can you help me?

I can.
I can.
I can.
We can help.

Oh, oh.
We see it.
We want it.

Not you.
Not you.
Not you.
Go away.
It is for my little baby and me.

Foundational Skills

In addition to reading the numerous high-frequency words in the text, this book also supports the development of foundational skills.

Phonological Awareness: The long i sound

Oddity Task: Say the long **i** sound (as in I or ice) for your child. Ask your child to say the word that has the long **i** sound in the following word groups:

bike, bin, bid	whiff, wife, win	in, fin, ice
sit, sip, side	pin, pen, pine	light, lit, let
red, rid, ride	chimp, champ, child	

Phonics: The letter Ii

1. Demonstrate how to form the letters **I** and **i** for your child.
2. Have your child practice writing **I** and **i** at least three times each.
3. Ask your child to point to the words in the book that begin with the letter **i**.
4. Write the words listed below on separate pieces of paper. Read each word aloud and ask your child to repeat them.

tie	rice	try	pie	sky	sigh
five	like	light	kind	nice	shy
high	fly	climb	night	ice	slide

5. Write the following long **i** spellings at the top of a piece of paper

   i   i_e   ie   igh

6. Ask your child to sort the words by placing them under the correct long **i** spelling.

Fluency: Echo Reading

1. Reread the story to your child at least two more times while your child tracks the print by running a finger under the words as they are read. Ask your child to read the words he or she knows with you.
2. Reread the story, stopping after each sentence or page to allow your child to read (echo) what you have read. Repeat echo reading and let your child take the lead.

Language

The concepts, illustrations, and text help children develop language both explicitly and implicitly.

Vocabulary: Personal Pronouns

1. Explain to your child that words that can be substituted for the names of people are called pronouns.
2. Write the following words on separate pieces of paper:

   I   me   he   she   we   you   they

3. Read each word to your child and ask your child to repeat it.
4. Mix the words up. Point to a word and ask your child to read it. Provide clues if your child needs them.
5. Read the following sentences to your child. Ask your child to provide an appropriate pronoun to complete the sentence.
   - The mother in the story is red. ___ is also little.
   - She asked the others, "Can ___ help me?"
   - The mother told the others to go away. She said, "Go away. It is for my baby and ___."
   - The others did not help. ___ did not work.
   - When the mother put the food out, the others said, "___ can help."

Reading Literature and Informational Text

To support comprehension, ask your child the following questions. The answers either come directly from the text or require inferences and discussion.

Key Ideas and Detail

- Ask your child to retell the sequence of events in the story.
- What is the mother getting on page 7?

Craft and Structure

- Is this a book that tells a story or one that gives information? How do you know?
- Why didn't the other three want to help the mother?

Integration of Knowledge and Ideas

- What kind of food would you feed a baby?
- What is the lesson in this story?

WORD LIST

Not I, Not I uses the 44 words listed below.

This list can be used to practice reading the words that appear in the text. You may wish to write the words on index cards and use them to help your child build automatic word recognition. Regular practice with these words will enhance your child's fluency in reading connected text.

a	help	oh	up
and	here	one	
away			want
	I	play	we
baby	in		where
big	is	red	work
	it	run	
can			yellow
come	little	said	you
	look	see	
down		something	
	make		
find	me	the	
for	Mother	three	
funny	my	to	
		two	
go	not		

ABOUT THE AUTHOR Margaret Hillert has helped millions of children all over the world learn to read independently. She was a first grade teacher for 34 years and during that time started writing books that her students could both gain confidence in reading and enjoy. She wrote well over 100 books for children just learning to read. As a child, she enjoyed writing poetry and continued her poetic writings as an adult for both children and adults.

Photograph by Glenna Washburn

ABOUT THE ILLUSTRATOR Bert Dodson is a painter, teacher, author and illustrator. He has illustrated over 80 books for children. He has also authored two books on drawing. In the 1980's he created the political comic strip, *Nuke*. He regularly exhibits his watercolors and drawings and for several years has been illustrating *Opera Stories for Children*, a series commissioned by The New York Metropolitan Opera. Bert resides in Vermont.